Claire's
Secret

Wendy Mortimer
Illustrated by David Cox

Rigby

Contents

1

An Unexpected Meeting

CLAIRE had been keeping a secret, a secret she didn't even tell her sister Tessie, in case Tessie told their parents.

It was hard keeping the secret, but she couldn't tell anyone. It would probably mean losing Jake. And she couldn't face that. She just couldn't.

Her mother and father had let her choose a pet for her birthday, as long as it wasn't anything large. She'd gone into the pet store hoping to find a kitten, or even a little white mouse.

Then she saw the large, colorful parrot. It was perched alone at the back of the shop. As she moved toward it, the bird winked one black, beady eye. Then it spoke:

"Higgledy dee,
look at me!"

Claire went closer.

The parrot spoke again:

"*Jake's the name,*

tricks are my game."

Wow! Claire had found what she wanted for her birthday, and she'd raced home to ask her mom and dad.

2

Jake's Tricks Begin

"**W**ELL," Claire's father said when they'd set Jake up on the back porch, "he sure is a fine-looking bird."

And he was. Jake had green, red, and blue feathers, and an orange beak. He was so tame, he didn't need to stay in a cage. He perched on a metal stand that had his seed and water cups attached to it.

Tessie, Claire's little sister, frowned. She didn't like the looks of Jake's hooked beak. She held her cat Matilda tightly, while Matilda struggled to get free.

"Wait till you hear him talk," Claire said, proudly. She whistled at the bird. "Say something, Jake."

Jake stared from one person to the next. Then he took a deep breath and drew himself up tall.

"Look, look, he's going to talk!" Claire said.

They all looked at Jake. He puffed out his chest and opened his beak. Then he screeched loudly—"SKAAAAAAAGH!"

Matilda leaped out of Tessie's arms and shot across the porch into the house.

5

Tessie giggled. "Yes, Claire, he can talk all right—*bird talk.*"

"He does so talk," Claire said. "Come on, Jake." She took Jake into the garden and set him down. Jake strutted around, scratching in the ground.

The dog next door must have heard them. "Woof!"

Jake put his beady eye to a crack in the fence.

"Woof!" the dog barked, louder.

"Woof! Woof! Woof! Woof!" growled Jake, in a perfect imitation of the dog's bark.

Claire fell back on her heels laughing. "Tessie, come and see this!" she called.

Tessie stepped out of the back door.

Jake stretched his wings, cleared his throat, and hissed quite clearly:

> "One, two, three,
>
> the dog's got a flea."

Now it was Tessie's turn to burst out laughing.

Claire turned to her sister. "Well, you believe me now, don't you?"

3

The Worst Day

JAKE soon showed himself to be a very clever bird. In no time, he learned to balance on the handlebars of Claire's bicycle. Everyday they went for a short ride. As soon as Jake saw Claire getting her bike out of the shed, he'd flap his wings and croak in his gravelly voice:

"*Hidey ho,*

let's go!"

But the day Claire saw the sign in the store window was one of the worst days of her life.

LOST
PET PARROT
TAME, FRIENDLY AND TALKS.
ANSWERS TO THE NAME OF JAKE.
PLEASE CALL JIM BAKER AT WORK:
555-1234

An awful feeling came over Claire when she read the sign. She quickly looked around, then she scratched at the tape and took the sign down. She scrunched it up and put it in her pocket. "Let's go, Jake!" she said.

It wasn't fair! It just wasn't fair!

All the way home, Claire's mind was racing. Perhaps it was a different bird, another bird named Jake! After all, they bought Jake from a pet shop, so he wasn't lost. Anyway, what if she hadn't even passed that shop, hadn't seen the sign?

That's it, she decided. She'd do nothing. Pretend she'd never even seen it.

But no matter how much she tried to convince herself, deep down she felt bad about keeping it a secret.

4

Show Off!

JAKE learned how to unclip the back screen door, so he came and went from his perch to the garden whenever he pleased. He soon picked up many more phrases, and in his funny voice, he copied everything. He made the sound of the phone ringing, the sound of the microwave "*ding*," and even the noise of the lawn mower!

Claire also taught Jake tricks. Jake loved performing.

Quite often, Claire thought of the sign for the lost parrot named Jake. Sometimes, she took the crumpled note from her drawer and smoothed it out to read again. But she never did anything about it. As much as she hated keeping the secret, she couldn't give Jake up now. He was the best pet in the whole world! Anyway, she told herself, look how happy Jake is!

It was true. Jake did love his new home. He loved the garden, the attention —he even loved Matilda and followed her around. And almost every day he went on a bike ride, balanced on Claire's handlebars. They never went far, but he would spread his wings as if he was flying, and you could tell he loved every moment.

5

An Offer Too Good to Refuse

ONE morning, Claire put Jake on her bike and headed toward the nearby playground. With Jake on her handlebars, as usual, she rode along, close to the sidewalk. Suddenly, she heard a loud noise just behind her. She turned her head and was startled to see a huge truck hurtling along the road, gaining on them.

As the slope they were on became steeper, Claire sped up. The truck was gathering speed! Its fumes made it hard for her to breathe, and the noise filled her ears.

There was a sudden loud honk as the driver sounded his horn.

The noise threw Claire off balance. She jerked the bike to one side, tipping it over. She and Jake hurtled into the air.

With a heavy thump and a roll, Claire landed on the ground. She watched the truck roar on by and disappear.

Right away, she looked for Jake.

The parrot was happily scratching around in the dirt.

"Phew!" Claire said aloud, her heart hammering. "That was close." She rubbed her sore ankle.

Just then a car pulled up. A man and woman got out, hurrying up to her.

"Are you hurt? We saw what happened! That truck *just* missed you!"

"Yes, we're okay, thanks," Claire said, brushing off her clothes.

The couple looked relieved.

"That's a fine-looking bird you have there," the man said to Claire.

Claire smiled as she stroked Jake's feathers. "He talks, too," she said.

The woman smiled. "We've seen you riding your bicycle around the neighborhood with your bird. You know, I work for a television station and I'm sure they'd be interested in you and your bird. How would you like to bring him along and appear on the children's program *Strange But True!* You could show us how you trained him, and let us hear him talk."

"I don't know."

"You'd be paid, of course—quite a lot, too. Why don't you ask your parents?"

"All right, I'll ask my mom and dad," Claire said.

"Great." The woman took a card from her pocket. "I'm Joan Kelly," she said. "Your parents can call me at the TV station if you decide to go ahead with it. I'll arrange everything. Well, bye now."

"Goodbye," the man said.

"Bye." Claire watched as they drove off.

She straightened her bike. "How about that!" she said. "We could be on TV!"

Jake flew to her, squawking.

"Higgledy dee,
look at me!
Jake's the name,
tricks are my game!"

As they rode home, Claire thought about it. She wasn't really worried that Jake's real owner would see the show because it was a daytime children's show. And maybe being on TV would be a lot of fun! The money would help her buy a big outdoor cage for Jake. Besides, she was sure Jake would enjoy himself.

But what would her parents say?

6

A Star Is Born

WOW! It was really happening. Her mom and dad had agreed. The arrangements were made, and soon the day for the TV show arrived.

Joan Kelly took Claire and Jake into the TV studio. Claire was surprised at how small it was—like a tiny theater. Microphones hung from the ceiling where huge round lights were set at all angles. Several TV cameras swiveled around the floor.

Claire felt as if fireworks were going off in her stomach.

"Now just relax," the interviewer said as he joined them. "I'm Perry Pingwell, but everyone calls me Oh Great One." He stared at Claire's puzzled face. "Only joking! Ha-ha-ha-ha."

Claire smiled, weakly.

"All right," Perry continued. "First I'll ask you about Jake, then we'll see if you can get him to do a few tricks, eh?"

Claire nodded.

"Now, when this red light is on, you're on camera, okay?"

Again Claire nodded. The rows of seats were full now and she faced a sea of people. Claire saw her mom and dad in the front row, and Tessie waving. It occurred to Claire that thousands of people would be watching her!

7

Lights, Camera, Action!

THE music for the *Strange But True!* program was playing. The lights blazed and Perry Pingwell was talking into one of the cameras. A camera zoomed up and Claire saw herself on the TV monitor.

Perry grinned into the camera. "Hello, boys and girls. Welcome to our program, *Strange But True!* This is Claire McDonald and her AMAZING pet parrot. All right, Claire, how about getting your bird to perform for us, eh?"

"Okay." Claire's voice came out in a whisper. "YES," she said again.

"Okay," said Perry, "let's see what you can do."

"Are you ready for some tricks, Jake?" asked Claire.

Jake answered:

> "Jake's the name,
>
> tricks are my game."

There was loud clapping from the audience.

Jake seemed to love the attention. He spoke again.

> "Jake's the name,
>
> and don't forget
>
> I'm the world's most amazing pet!"

"Jake," Claire said, "show your wings."

Jake spread his wings wide and flapped them a little.

26

"Do you like lemonade?"

At this, Jake dipped his head and swayed around.

"What about medicine?"

Jake shook himself all over and made a noise like "AAARGH."

Everybody was laughing. "This is going pretty well!" Claire thought. She began to relax a little. "Scare the robber, Jake," she told the bird.

Jake drew himself up to his full height, spread his wings, and barked. He sounded just like a big dog.

But even when the clapping stopped, Jake kept barking and growling.

27

Next Jake made a shrill noise like the telephone ringing, followed by a screech that sounded like tires squealing.

He was enjoying himself, and he wasn't going to stop.

"That's enough. Take a bow, Jake," Claire said.

Jake lifted one wing, bent his head down, and swept his wing around in front of himself, bowing low.

"Well," said Perry Pingwell, "you're a clever bird, all right." He poked a finger into Jake's chest. "How about talking for Perry," he said. "Polly want a cracker?"

Jake remained silent.

"Jake want a cracker? Jake want a cracker?" Perry chanted, trying to get Jake to talk.

But Jake was staring at the microphone above their heads.

"Polly want a cracker?" croaked Jake, and he suddenly leaped up, grabbed the dangling microphone, and swung on it.

The audience laughed loudly.

That was when Perry Pingwell made his big mistake. He tried to grab Jake. Jake screeched, grabbed a beakful of the man's hair, and twisted sharply.

"AAARGH" Perry groaned, right into the microphone so that the sound of his cry was as loud as a plane taking off.

"Jake, let go!" Claire shouted.

Jake did let go, but immediately grabbed Perry's tie instead, and yanked.

In the next instant, the studio lights went off.

8

The Confession

AT breakfast the next day, Claire's mom showed her the newspaper. "Claire, you've made the papers. There's a little story about you and Jake on the show. Look."

Claire read the story.

Her stomach felt all squishy. Oh, no! What if her secret came out? She was already worried that Jake's real owner might have seen her on TV, even though it was a daytime children's show. Now, the story was in the paper, too.

Claire frowned. It had been so hard keeping the secret of the sign for the lost parrot named Jake. It was wrong, she knew, to keep a pet who belonged to somebody else. She wasn't very proud of herself.

And she knew what she had to do.

"Mom and Dad, there's something I have to tell you," Claire said. "It's important." She went to her room and took the crumpled piece of paper from her drawer. She smoothed it out and showed her mom. "It was in a store window," Claire said. "After I'd read it, I ... I took it."

Her mother read the sign.

When she'd finished reading, she shook her head. "You should have told us right from the start, Claire."

Claire nodded.

"I know I should have. It's been awful keeping it a secret."

"Well, you've done the right thing by telling us now," her mom said. "Better late than never." She ruffled Claire's hair. "It's hard, I know," she went on, "but of course, we have to call this man and tell him we've got his bird."

That was just what Claire was afraid of. "I know," she said. "But it might be a different bird. Maybe there's another parrot named Jake. I mean, he wasn't lost. We bought him from the pet store."

Her mother shook her head. "Probably somebody found the parrot and took him to the pet store and the owner then put him up for sale."

Claire's stomach felt as if it was going around in a washing machine. She knew her mom was right. There was only one thing for Claire to do now.

"We'll get another pet," her father said.

Claire didn't answer. She took Jake on her arm and went outside. Jake began scratching around in the garden.

Claire watched him, blinking back her tears. She stayed there for a long time.

When she came inside again, her mom spoke in a gentle voice. "Don't put it off, Claire."

Claire picked up the phone.

9

Goodbye ...
and a New Start

THAT night, Claire had a glass of milk but couldn't eat her dinner. She sat, pushing the food around on her plate. She was glad she didn't have to keep her secret anymore, but now the very thing she'd been afraid of—losing Jake—was going to come true.

"May I leave the table?" she asked.

Her father nodded. Claire went out to the porch. Jake was standing on one leg, his feathers ruffled. He was sound asleep. But Claire whispered to him anyway.

"You're the best pet in the world," she said. "I won't ever forget you." She couldn't say anymore because her throat had somehow closed up.

Next morning, as soon as Claire woke up, she felt as if a giant hand was squeezing her heart. It was the day Jake's owner was coming to get him. She went to the porch, took Jake on her shoulder, and returned to her bedroom. Jake seemed now to sense that something was wrong.

Claire heard the front doorbell.

She turned to Jake and scratched his chest feathers. "I think this is goodbye, Jake," she whispered.

There was a quiet knock on the door.

Her dad came in, followed by a tall, thin man with a friendly face.

"Hello, Claire," Jim Baker said. His eyes went to the parrot. "Well, hidey ho, my old friend!"

With an excited squawk, Jake flew and landed on Mr. Baker's shoulder. "Oh, you remember me, do you?" Mr. Baker asked, giving the parrot's feathers a scratch.

Claire's heart sank to her feet.

"I'm sorry I didn't let you know sooner," Claire told Mr. Baker. "But I've taken good care of him. I always give him fresh seed and water and treats."

"I can see he is well taken care of," said Mr. Baker.

Claire went on. "And I take him outside and he never flies away. He usually comes with me on my bike. I've taught him tricks and lots of new phrases. He really likes it here. Don't you, Jake?"

Jake's eyes danced.

"Well, I'm thrilled to hear all this," Mr. Baker said, "because I'm moving out of the country next week. And, of course, I can't take Jake with me."

"Out of the country!" Claire repeated.

"Yes, I have a new job to go to. That's why I took Jake to a friend's place to live. It seems Jake didn't like it there and he flew away. I've been trying ever since then to find him, to make sure he had a good home."

Claire's heart began to thump.

"So he's your bird now, Claire. What do you think of that?" Mr. Baker finished.

"Oh, Mr. Baker, thanks!" shouted Claire. She leaped up and shook his hand.

Her dad shook hands with Mr. Baker, too, while Jake bobbed his head and squawked.

"I'll send you pictures of Jake," promised Claire.

"And I'll send you a postcard from France," Mr. Baker said.

Claire held out her arm. "Here, Jake," she called.

Jake flew to her, landing on her shoulder. Puffing out his feathers, the parrot spoke in his funny, gravelly voice:

> *"Jake's the name,*
> *and don't forget!"*

And everybody chanted together:

> *"You're the world's most amazing pet!"*

Jake drew himself up tall and looked around, his head nodding and dipping in agreement.

Then he winked one black, beady eye.